Tat

Written by Fiona Undrill

Illustrated by Louise Forshaw

Collins

Dan sits in.

2

Sit in it.

dip dip dip

Dip in it.

Pam taps it.

tap tap tap

a sad man

Nip at it.

nap nap nap

pad pad pad

Pad in tins.

14

 After reading

Letters and Sounds: Phase 2

Word count: 36

Focus phonemes: /s/ /a/ /t/ /p/ /i/ /n/ /m/ /d/

Curriculum links: Expressive arts and design

Early learning goals: Reading: use phonic knowledge to decode regular words and read them aloud accurately

Developing fluency

- Your child may enjoy hearing you read the book.
- Encourage your child to read the text with expression. For example, add a sad tone for a sad man on page 8 and a lively tone for a mad mat on page 10.

Phonic practice

- Turn to page 8 and point to the word **man**. Ask your child to sound out and blend the letters in the word. (m/a/n – **man**) Turn to page 10 and repeat for **mad**. (m/a/d – **mad**)
- On pages 2 and 6, focus on the children's names, **Dan** and **Pam**. Ask your child to sound out and blend each, checking they don't muddle the sounds /n/ in **Dan** and /m/ in **Pam**.
- Look at the "I spy sounds" pages (14–15). Point to and sound out the /m/ at the top of page 14, then point to the musical notes and say "music", emphasising the /m/ sound. Ask your child to find other things that start with the /m/ sound. (*maracas, mat, mum, milk bottle, mess, matchbox, microphone*). Next ask them what else they can see, and to listen for which words have the /m/ sound in the middle or end. (*hammer, drum, strum, thump, broom*)

Extending vocabulary

- Turn to pages 10–11. Ask your child: What other words could you use to describe the cat's mad mat? (e.g. *crazy, colourful, patchwork, funny, wacky, pretty, comfy*)